Daisy Dawson

on the Farm

Steve Voake

illustrated by Jessica Meserve

**WALKER
BOOKS**

First published 2012 by Walker Books Ltd
87 Vauxhall Walk, London SE11 5HJ

2 4 6 8 10 9 7 5 3 1

Text © 2012 Steve Voake
Illustrations © 2012 Jessica Meserve

This book has been typeset in StempelSchneidler

Printed and bound in Great Britain by Clays Ltd, St Ives plc

British Library Cataloguing in Publication Data:
a catalogue record for this book is available from the British Library

ISBN 978-1-4063-2748-9

www.walker.co.uk

For Freya & Louis
S.V.

For Elodie & Rowan
J.M.

Heat and Dust

Everyone said that this summer was hotter than anyone could remember. Grass turned from green to brown, rolling rivers became tiny streams and everyone slept with their windows open. In every shop and on every street corner, people discussed the weather. In every field and on every farm, animals discussed it too, although most people couldn't understand them. But Daisy Dawson could, and at this moment she was standing in the lane listening to a spider talk about flies.

"It's been a good year for them," said the spider. "I've eaten four this morning and there's another twenty-seven in the larder."

"That's a lot of flies," said Daisy.

"I know," agreed the spider. "You want some?"

"No thanks," said Daisy. And then because she didn't want to appear rude she added, "It's very kind, but I've just had some Honey Nut Loops."

"Bumblebees, you mean," replied the spider. "Tasty little critters, aren't they?"

Daisy was about to explain that she didn't eat bumblebees for breakfast when she saw Boom the dog padding across the field towards her.

"Uh-oh!" said the spider, scurrying off into the hedge. "It's the big bad barky thing!"

Daisy was still giggling when Boom reached the gate.

"What's so funny?" he asked.

"That spider," explained Daisy. "She just called you a big bad barky thing."

Boom growled and tried to look fierce, which made Daisy laugh even more.

"I'm sorry, Boom," she said. "I'm afraid you're just not very good at being cross."

"Unlike the animals on the farm, then," replied Boom.

"What do you mean?"

"I mean that the pigs are arguing with the chickens, the donkeys are sad because the hot weather reminds them of the beach and the ducks and newts are miserable because their pond has dried up."

He closed one eye and squinted up at her in the bright sunshine.

"I don't suppose you know any rain dances, do you?"

Daisy smiled.

"I'll see what I can do," she said.

Rocky the Bull

When they got to the bridge the cows were all standing in the river, trying to keep cool.

"My joints ache something dreadful," said Doris.

"That's the rheumatism," replied Phyllis. "Comes from standing in all this water."

"How come Rocky never gets it?" asked Doris, staring at an enormous black bull who was sitting peacefully in the shade.

"He's got a copper ring through his nose," said Mavis, flicking her tail at some flies. "Does wonders for it, apparently."

As Boom sniffed at a patch of wild strawberries, Daisy leant on the handrail of the little bridge and gazed down at the cool, clear water. She had never heard cows talking before and decided that she would like to stay and listen for a while.

"I think Rocky's lovely," said Freya, who was one of the younger cows.

"He's a dreamboat," agreed Erica.

"I think," said Phyllis, "that someone has a crush on someone else."

"No I haven't," said Freya and Erica together. Then they both looked at each other and burst out laughing.

As Boom raised his eyes skywards, Daisy whispered, "Look. Rocky's coming over."

"Yoo-hoo," called Erica. "Yoo-hoo, Rocky!"

Rocky stood on the bank and put a hoof next to his ear.

"Was that the sound of an angel?" he asked. "Or was it the stars falling down from the sky?"

"It was neither of those things!" squealed Erica happily. "It was me, Rocky. It was me!"

"Then I was right the first time," said Rocky.

"Oh *stop* it," giggled Erica.

"Yes, stop it," agreed Boom.

"Oh, hey there, Dog." Rocky waved a hoof at Boom and then turned his attention to Daisy. "And who's the little lady come trimp-tramping over my bridge?"

"I'm Daisy," replied Daisy.

"Well of course you are," said Rocky. "The most beautiful flower in all the meadow."

"Pay no attention to him," said Boom. "He's always like this."

"I don't mind," said Daisy, who rather liked being called a beautiful flower. She looked down at the cows standing in the cool water, then back at Rocky, who seemed happy in the hot sun.

"Doesn't the heat bother you at all?" she asked.

"No ma'am," said Rocky, "and you want to know why?"

"Not really," said Boom.

"Yes please!" said Freya and Erica together.

"Then let me tell you about it," replied Rocky. And to Daisy's surprise, he started dancing up and down the riverbank, moving his shoulders and crossing his hooves this way and that. And as he moved, the cows hummed and bobbed their heads up and down to the rhythm of his song.

"When the world is smoking hot
You gotta make sure that you are not.
Lady-cows, take my advice:
You gotta stay cool like the snow and ice.
So do the dance and sing the song,
You can do it short or you can do it long,
But if you do it like Rocky then you
    can't go wrong
'Cos that's how you do the
    ice-cool song."

"The ice-cool song, the
ice-cool song, that's how you do
the ice-cool song," echoed the cows.

"All *right!*" said Rocky, doing a two-step
and twirling around to face the river again.
"Now *that's* what I'm talkin' 'bout!"

As Daisy clapped and danced her way
across the bridge, the cows mooed and Rocky
nodded his head, tapping his hooves in the
dust. When she reached the other side he was
sitting in the long grass, waiting for her.

"Daisy, you've got the rhythm of nature,"
he said. "No doubt about it."

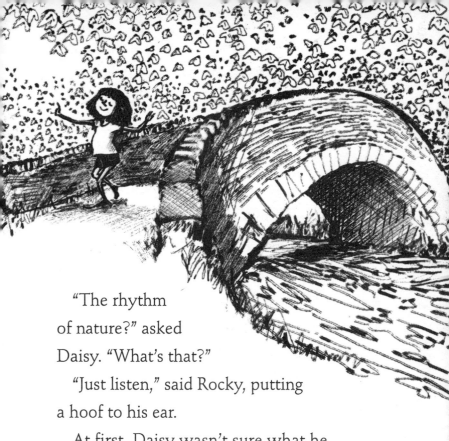

"The rhythm
of nature?" asked
Daisy. "What's that?"

"Just listen," said Rocky, putting
a hoof to his ear.

At first, Daisy wasn't sure what he
meant. But then she heard the humming
of the bees, the whisper of the wind and
the rattle of the stones as the river made its
slow, unhurried progress towards the sea.
And as she listened again, she heard the
creak of the branches and the soft beating
of her heart.

"You see?" said Rocky. "The rhythm of nature is all around you. And what's more, it's inside you too. It's what makes a tree a tree and a daisy a daisy."

He pointed his hoof at Daisy and winked.

"And what could be better than that?"

As Daisy walked with Boom across the meadow towards the farm, she heard the swish of the grass beneath her feet and the song of the birds in the hedgerows. She also heard a softer, lower sound and realized that it was Boom, humming a little tune.

"Boom," she said. "Are you singing the ice-cool song?"

"Maybe."

"Well, perhaps if you keep going it will make the rain come," said Daisy, skipping along beside him. "Perhaps it could be our very own rain dance."

Boom looked up at the blue sky.

"Well, it's not a very good one," he said, "because it's not working. But at least Martha will be pleased it's not raining."

"Martha?" asked Daisy. "Who's Martha?"

"She's a pig," explained Boom, "and I'm sure she would love to meet you."

Pigs and Chickens

When they reached the farm Daisy let Boom
into the yard before closing the gate behind
her. Two grey donkeys were standing next
to an old barn stacked high with golden
hay bales, and a family of ducks lay asleep
in the shade, their heads tucked under their
wings. A rust-coloured chicken pecked
at a few seeds scattered in the dust and,
somewhere in the distance, a wood pigeon
cooed soft and low. Daisy was just starting

to think how peaceful everything was when a small piglet stuck his head through the metal gate next to the pigpens. He looked at her for a moment, then began moving his head up and down so that the gate went *clangety-clang-clang-clang.*

"I'm bored," he said. "I'm bored, bored, bored, bored, *bored.*"

"Pauly Piglet, do you *have* to do that?" asked his mother Martha, trotting out of her pigsty.

"I don't have to, but I wanna," said Pauly, moving his head so that the gate went *clangety-clang-clang-clang* again.

"I bet I'm boreder than you are," said his brother Pete, snuffling at a patch of dried mud by the wall.

"More bored, you mean," said his mother.

"Whatever," said Pete. "Anyway, there's nothing interesting to do around here."

"It's all the chickens' fault," said Patsy Piglet. "If they weren't so lazy, we wouldn't be so hot and bothered."

"I *squawk* your pardon!" spluttered Doreen Chicken, spitting seeds against a watering can with a loud *f-tang!* "Who are you calling lazy?"

"I didn't say *you* were lazy," replied Patsy. "I said *all* chickens were lazy."

"That's even worse!" squawked Doreen.

"Fascinating though this conversation is," said Boom, "I think I'm going to go and have a lie-down."

As he wandered off towards the barn, Daisy crouched down and patted Doreen on the head. "Chickens aren't lazy," she said. "They lay eggs and make clucking noises. And sometimes they go for little walks."

"At last," said Doreen, "someone who understands."

"No, listen," said Patsy. "You used to stand on our backs and flap your wings and it was lovely and cool. But now you've stopped."

"That isn't because we're lazy," said Doreen. "It's because we're hot."

"But flappy wings cool you down," said Pete.

"They cool *you* down, you mean," replied Doreen.

"Us, you. Who's counting?" said Pete.

Clangety-clang-clang-clang went the gate.

"Pauly, *please*," said Martha. She looked at Daisy and shook her head. "I'm sorry about this, dear. I'm afraid everyone's rather bad-tempered, what with the heat and all. But to be honest, I'm glad it's not raining. At least I'm not cleaning up muddy trotter-prints every five minutes. I can keep the house tidy at last."

"House?" asked Daisy, glancing at the pigsty.

"Oh I know it's not much to most folks, but it's home to me. Why don't you step inside and have a look around?"

Boom seemed quite happy over by the hay bales, so Daisy followed Martha into the pigsty. To her surprise she saw that there were hundreds of wild flowers poking out from the cracks in the walls; dog rose and dandelion were bundled with comfrey and cornflower, filling the place with perfume and colour. At the base of the walls were neat piles of carrots, potatoes, turnips and onions. Each pile had a picture of the vegetable scratched into the dust in front of it.

"Oh Martha, these are lovely!" exclaimed Daisy, clasping her hands together. "Wherever did you find them?"

"Oh I picked them up here and there," replied Martha, neatening up the edges of the onion pile. "I saved them from the trough and so on. But to tell you the truth, it's Pandora who does most of the decorating."

Daisy frowned.

"Pandora? Who's Pandora?"

"That's me," said a little voice from the corner of the sty. "Would you like to come and see my drawings?"

Daisy turned to see a small piglet waving her trotter.

She smiled and waved back.

"I'd *love* to see your drawings," she said.

"This one isn't finished yet," said Pandora, trotting out of the corner so that Daisy could get a better look. "I need to draw more ducks."

As Daisy got closer she saw that Pandora had scratched a picture of a meadow with a duck pond in the middle. It was beautifully drawn, but the best thing about it was the colours. Pandora had used petals, leaves and vegetable peelings to bring it to life and the duck pond had been sprinkled with blue cornflowers to make it look as though it was full of water.

"It's wonderful, Pandora," said Daisy. "How did you learn to draw so beautifully?"

"I just love doing it," replied Pandora, "and that seems to teach me all by itself."

"But you've drawn the duck pond with water in it," said Martha. "Everyone knows that the duck pond is all dried up."

"I know," said Pandora, "but I don't just draw things the way they are. I draw them the way I *want* them to be."

Daisy was about to add a few more petals to Pandora's picture when there was a squawk from the yard and then a small voice quacked, "Please, Daisy, can you come and help us? We really, *really* want our pond back."

Pond Plans

"All right, everybody!" called Daisy, standing on top of the hay bales and clapping her hands together. "If we're going to get this sorted out, then we need to listen to each other. And first of all, you need to listen to me."

When everyone was silent, Daisy realized that she wasn't sure what she was going to say next. But when she saw the sad faces of the animals staring up at her and the tiny newts sitting glumly in the dust, she knew she would have to find a way of cheering them up.

"Now I know you're fed up with the heat," she said, "and I know…" – here she glanced at the donkeys – "that some of you are missing the seaside. But I'm sure that if we all work together, we can find a way of making things better."

There were low murmurs of agreement as the animals looked at one another and nodded. Daisy saw the ducks waving at her and remembered why she had got all the animals together in the first place.

"As you all know," she went on, "the biggest problem is the dried-up duck pond. The ducks don't have anywhere to swim and the newts don't have anywhere to live. So that means we all need to put our thinking-caps on. Does anyone have any good ideas?"

"Hmm," said Hoofy the donkey, blinking in the bright sunlight. "Perhaps we could take them to the seaside. It's awfully nice there, you know."

"That's a lovely thought," said Daisy, "but I'm afraid the seaside is probably a bit too far away."

"Too far away," echoed the other donkey, whose name was Straw. "Far too far away…"

As Doreen Chicken patted his leg sympathetically, a familiar voice called out, "Why don't we fill the pond up with water?"

"Hooray!" quacked the ducks. "Fill the pond up with water!"

"I don't think it's as easy as that," said Daisy.

"Not as easy as that," quacked the ducks.

"But it *is* easy," said the voice.

Daisy peered down and saw a small squirrel with its arms folded, sitting next to the chickens.

"Conker?" she said. "Is that you?"

"Well it was the last time I checked," replied Conker.

Daisy heard the sound of giggling and saw Conker's sister Hazel standing next to him with a paw over her mouth. When she saw Daisy she waved and then giggled again because Conker was flapping his arms and strutting around like a chicken.

"Me like corn," he said. "Me lay eggy-weggs."

One of the chickens stuck her foot out and Conker tripped over it, tumbling to the ground.

"Ow," he said, rubbing his head. "Me go crashy-crash."

When he saw the chickens glaring at him he got up and took a few steps backwards.

"Like I said," he went on, "all we need is to fill the pond up with water."

"Fill it up!" quacked the ducks. "Fill it up! Fill it up!"

"That's all very well," said Daisy, "but how do we do it?"

"Easy," said Conker. "Easy-peasy lemon squeezy. Or rather, easy-peasy, *voley* squeezy."

The chickens looked at one another.

"*Voley* squeezy?"

"That's what I said."

"This may sound like a silly question," said Daisy, "but what on earth is *voley* squeezy?"

"Water voles," said Conker. "Whenever I go down to the riverbank, they always shake their coats on me and I get soaking wet. They think it's really funny." He sniggered. "So do I, actually."

"Your point being?" asked Doreen Chicken, who was still slightly annoyed by Conker's chicken impression.

"All we need to do is get the voles soaking wet and then wring them out in the duck pond. And there you have it. Problem solved."

"Hooray!" quacked the ducks. "Problem solved!"

"I don't know," said Daisy. "I'm not sure those little voles will want to be dragged from the river and squeezed out in the middle of a duck pond."

"Trust me, they'll love it," said Conker.

"They're always game for a laugh, aren't they, Haze?"

Hazel nodded. "Remember when they played skimmies across the water?"

"Now that *was* funny," said Conker. "They found an elastic band, stretched it between two branches and fired themselves across the river. Vincent bounced seventeen times before he hit a tree, didn't he, Haze?"

"And twice more when he fell back in the water."

"Good times," said Conker.

"I think the squirrel might be onto something," said Maureen Chicken, who, unlike her sister Doreen, had secretly found Conker's chicken impression quite entertaining.

"The newts could go for a swim in the water trough while they're waiting," suggested Pauly Piglet.

"That is, if Hoofy and Straw don't mind."

"Don't mind at all," said Hoofy.

"Glad to be of service," said Straw.

"Thank you," said Daisy. "And thank *you*, Pauly. That was a really helpful suggestion."

Pauly was so pleased with himself that he completely forgot about clanging his head in the gate and went off to find some stones to put in the water trough, so it would feel more like home to the newts.

"So what are we doing again?" asked Doreen.

"Teasing moles," said Noreen, who was Doreen's eldest sister and rather hard of hearing. "And putting boots in the water trough."

"Squeezing voles," Daisy corrected her. "And putting *newts* in the water trough."

"Exactly," said Noreen. "That's what I said."

Daisy sighed and looked at Hoofy and Straw. "Why don't you two take the ducks

and newts over to the water trough?
The pigs and squirrels can come to the river
with me."

"What about us?" asked the chickens.
"What can we do?"

"You," said Daisy, "can do a very special
… other job."

"Which is?" asked the chickens, wings on
their hips.

Daisy thought quickly.

"A rain dance."

The chickens looked at one another.

"A rain dance?"

"Yes, you know. In case squeezing voles isn't quite enough. Then maybe the rain will fill the duck pond, water the fields and bring lots of juicy worms wriggling to the surface."

"Ooh, I like the sound of that," said Doreen. "I like the sound of that a *lot*."

"So let me get this straight," said Shakira Chicken: "we just make up a dance and if it's a really good one then it will rain?"

"Well, I've never done it before," Daisy admitted, "but you never know. It might just work."

"Alrighty then," said Doreen, flapping her wings. "One rain dance coming up."

"I see your wings are working again," said Patsy Piglet. "Funny that."

"Come on," said Daisy, steering Patsy away before she started another argument. "Let's go down to the river. We've got work to do."

Voley Squeezy

"There's Vince," said Conker, pointing his paw at the far side of the river. Sitting at the entrance to a small hole in the bank was a tiny water vole. When he saw Conker he waved, jumped into the water and paddled across the river towards them.

"He's a good swimmer," said Hazel. "Can't climb trees though."

"I can't swim *or* climb trees," said Boom sadly.

"But you can bark," said Daisy.

"I can, can't I?" said Boom more cheerfully. And just to prove it, he threw his head back and barked at exactly the same moment that Vince Vole was starting to climb up the bank.

"Yikes!" cried Vince, clutching his chest and falling back into the river.

"Vince!" called Conker. "Are you OK?"

Vince dragged himself up the bank, lay on his back and blew out a mouthful of water.

"No problem," he said. "Minor setback." He opened one eye and looked up at Daisy. "And who have we here, might I ask?"

"You already know Hazel and the pigs," said Conker. "And this here is Daisy Dawson."

Vince sat up and looked at her more closely.

"Are you the talking girl that everyone keeps telling me about?"

"Yes she is," said Conker before Daisy could answer. "She talks to squirrels and voles and everything."

"I can't bark though," said Daisy, who wanted to make sure that Boom didn't feel left out.

"Glad to hear it," said Vince. "If you'd both had a go I might never have got out of the water."

Boom barked once more as a joke and when Vince clutched his chest and pretended to fall over again, Pauly Piglet laughed so much that he got the hiccups and had to run down to the river for a drink.

"So tell me, Daisy Dawson," said Vince when everyone had stopped laughing, "what brings you here with old Conky? He hasn't dropped his lunch in the water again, has he?"

"It's the duck pond actually," said Daisy. "It's all dried up and there's nowhere for the ducks and newts to swim."

"Why don't they swim in the river?" asked Vince. "There's plenty of room for everyone."

"Newts don't like running water," said Daisy. "And anyway, the ducks have always lived on the pond. It's their home."

"Ah well, I suppose I can understand that," said Vince, looking fondly at the river.

"So how can I help?"

"We want you to be a sponge," said Conker.

"Huh?" said Vince.

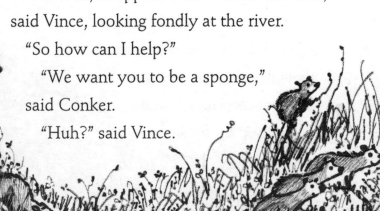

"We want you to soak up as much water as you can from the river," explained Daisy. "Then we'll take you over to the duck pond and wring you out."

"Like this," said Hazel, twisting her paws together and making small sucky noises.

"Hmm," said Vince. "Interesting."

Turning around to face the river, he put his paws in his mouth and blew. There was a high-pitched whistle and immediately hundreds of little faces appeared up and down the riverbank, whiskers twitching as they waited to find out why Vincent Vole had used the Waterside Whistle.

"Your countryside needs you, people!" Vince called, cupping his paws around his mouth. "Soak up the rain juice and head for the duck pond!"

The moment he had finished speaking, the river was alive with splashes as voles hugged their knees and jumped into the water. It looked just as if someone had thrown a thousand small stones into the water all at once.

"Wow!" cried Hazel and Conker together. "Fantastic!"

Once all the voles had swum to the bank, Daisy led the way across the bridge with two medium-sized voles balanced on her shoulders and a very small one, whose name was Littlest Vole, standing on her head.

"Squeezy peasy!" he squeaked, hopping from foot to foot. *"Squeezy peasy!"*

"You be careful up there, Littlest Vole," said Daisy. "We don't want you falling off." Behind her, another group of voles were riding on the backs of Boom and the three pigs while Hazel and Conker led hundreds more across the bridge.

"Hurry up, everyone!" called Vince, standing on Boom's back with steam rising from his fur. "We have to reach the pond before the sun dries us out!"

"Hold on tight!" Daisy cried. Then she took a deep breath and started to run.

"Yay-hey-hey!" cried Littlest Vole, hanging on to her hair and bouncing up and down. "This is the best day ever!"

When they all reached the pond, Hoofy and Straw were nibbling at the dry grass around the edge and the ducks were staring up at the sky.

"No sign of any rain yet," said Dave Duck.

"You said that five minutes ago," replied Kevin.

"All right," said Dave. "Don't bust your beak."

When they saw Daisy they flapped their wings and waddled across to meet her.

"All right, Daisy?" said Dave. "How's it going?"

"So far, so good," replied Daisy as the

voles gathered at the edge of the pond.
"If it doesn't work, it won't be for the want
of trying."

"OK, listen up, everyone," said Vince,
climbing up onto Boom's head. "What
we have here is a Dry Pond Situation. But
thanks to Conker's quick thinking, we also
have a Wet Vole Solution. Daisy, if you
wouldn't mind?"

Daisy put the other voles down on the
grass and then lifted Vince up into the air.

"Woah, that was a bit fast," said Vince,
shaking his head. "Made the old brain spin a
bit there."

"Sorry," said Daisy.

Vince shut his eyes for a moment, then
opened them again.

"No problem," he said. "Minor setback."

Daisy took him to the middle of the dried-
up pond while all the other animals stood
and watched.

"And now," Vince announced, raising his arms up in the air, "let the wringing commence!"

"Hooray!" cried the animals.

"Are you sure?" whispered Daisy.

"Of course I'm sure!" replied Vince.

Daisy put her hands around Vince's middle, turned him sideways and held him out over the dry earth.

"And ... squeeze!" said Vince.

As Daisy gently twisted her hands together, Vince squeaked

"Eeeeeee-ooooh-chee-yow!" and two tiny drops of water splashed to earth.

"Again," said Vince, his voice slightly higher than before.

Daisy took a deep breath and twisted her

hands together again. *"Eeeeeee-ooooh-chee-yow-chee-ooh!"* squeaked Vince again. Then he added, "Reckon that ought to do it."

As all the other animals ran over to have a look, Vince sucked on his teeth and stared at the dry ground.

Dave Duck shook his head.

"Can't see myself swimming in that, to be honest."

"Maybe the rest of us should have a go," piped up Littlest Vole.

"Yes, let's!" cried the others.

They quickly got into pairs and there was lots of giggling and squeaking as they all took it in turns to squeeze each other's fur. When they had finished, they stood back and looked at where they had hoped a pond full of water might be. But instead there was only a patch of damp earth, which was already beginning to dry out in the midday sun.

"All right, everyone," shouted Vince, clenching his paw above his head. "What is it that voles never do?"

"Crossword puzzles!" cried Littlest Vole, who had heard someone talking about them on a picnic.

"Dance with foxes!" shouted another.

"No, no, no," said Vince, shaking his head. "It's give up. Voles never give up!"

"NEVER!" cried the other voles. "NEVER GIVE UP!"

"I was going to say that next," whispered Littlest Vole. "I definitely was."

"To the river!" shouted Vince.

"TO THE RIVER!" cried the other voles.

"TO THE RIVER! TO THE RIVER!"

As the voles ran back across the meadow, Pauly Piglet looked up at the sky and shook his head. "I wish it would rain," he said.

"Me too," said Pete. "Just think of all that lovely mud."

"Don't you think it's odd," said Daisy, "that whenever you want it to rain, it doesn't, and whenever you don't, it does?"

"What do you mean?" asked Hazel.

"I heard my teacher saying the other day that it can be sunny for ages and ages, but whatever day they choose for the School Fete, it always pours with rain. And it's the same with Village Day."

"What's Village Day?" asked Conker.

"It's when the whole village comes together and they have singing and dancing and games and races. But Miss Frink says she always takes an umbrella because they usually end up packing away in the rain."

"Maybe we should have a Farm Day, then!" said Pauly Pig.

"Don't be daft," said Patsy. "We've got enough to do trying to fill up the duck pond."

"No, you don't understand," said Pauly. "I mean, if we organize a special Farm Afternoon and pretend we really want dry weather, then maybe the weather will hear us and decide that it's going to rain."

Daisy smiled.

"I'm not sure if it *always* works that way," she said, "but it's worth a try. So come on, everyone. What are we waiting for? Let's get ready for the best Farm Afternoon ever!"

Dancing Chickens

As the animals gathered together outside the barn waiting for the Farm Afternoon to start, Daisy sat on the hay bales next to Boom and watched Doreen Chicken bossing the other chickens about.

"Don't stand like that, you daft bird!" she squawked as a small chicken turned to face the opposite way from all the others. "How could you possibly think that was the right way round?"

"She seems a bit upset," said Daisy as Doreen fussed around making sure all the chickens were facing in the same direction. "How's the rain dance going?"

"They've been practising all morning," said Hazel.

"And arguing too," said Conker as Doreen finally got the chickens into a neat row across the middle of the farmyard.

"Chickens are very temperamental," said Pauly Pig.

"What's *temperamental* mean?" asked Pete.

"It means they can be up one minute and down the next," explained Patsy.

"Like rabbits," said Pete. "Boing! Boing! Boing!"

"All right, everyone!" shouted Doreen Chicken, dancing around and clapping her wings above her head. "Come on! Wooh! Yeah!"

As everyone turned to look,

the chickens started moving their feet up
and down and then began to sing,

"We're chickens, oh we're chickens
We're down on the farm doing no one no harm
We're just chickens, yeah we're chickens
We've got more sense than those battery hens

Strutting out across the yard
We think we're so lucky-luck-lucky
And they're going to find it hard
To turn us into Kentucky-tuck-tucky

'Cos we're chickens, oh we're chickens
We're down on the farm doing no one no harm
We're just chickens, yeah we're chickens
We've got more sense than those battery hens!"

Boom tapped his paws, Daisy put her arms around the two swaying donkeys and the squirrels danced around the hay bales with the piglets.

"Break it down!" shouted Doreen, and all the chickens went,

>*"Cluck, cluckety-cluck, SQUAWK!*
>*Cluck, cluckety-cluck, SQUAWK!"*

Then Doreen danced over to where Daisy was sitting and beckoned her over with her wing.

"Me?" mouthed Daisy, pointing at herself.

"Yes, come along, my dear," squawked Doreen. "Come and join our dance!"

Daisy felt a bit nervous at first, but then she remembered what Rocky the bull had said about the rhythm of nature, and as the squirrels danced, the donkeys brayed and the piglets clapped their trotters together, she jumped off the hay bales and skipped over to join the chickens in the middle of the yard.

"What do I do?" she giggled as the chickens danced around her and the animals cheered.

"Just watch me," squawked Doreen, "and a one, two, three, wings up!"

As the chickens raised their wings, Daisy put up her arms and waved her hands in the air.

"Like this?" she asked.

"That's it!" squawked Doreen. "Now flap to the beat!"

Wiggling her elbows back and forth, Daisy made sure that she kept in time with the chickens as they flapped their wings and lifted their feet up and down to the rhythm. While they were all fanning out into a long line, she glanced over towards the field and saw Rocky and the cows watching her from beside the water trough.

"Shake those feathers, Daisy Dawson!" bellowed Rocky, standing on one leg and spinning around in a circle. "Show those chickens how to dance!"

Daisy giggled and then held her hands out in front of her, spinning them around as if she was gathering up an imaginary ball of wool. When the chickens saw this they clucked with delight and soon they were all doing the same thing with their wings. Daisy felt a wave of happiness wash over her. Although she had been worried about joining in at first, now that she was dancing it felt like

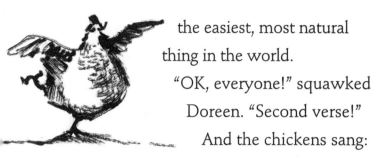

the easiest, most natural
thing in the world.

"OK, everyone!" squawked
Doreen. "Second verse!"
And the chickens sang:

*"We do our rain dance out across the yard
And we go clucky-cluck-clucky
'Cos an empty pond is hard
If you're a ducky-duck-ducky*

*So we're dancin' and we're prancin'
We're down on the farm doing no one no harm."*

"Everybody!" shouted Doreen, clapping
her wings together.

*"We're just dancin' and we're prancin'
We're down on the farm doing
no one no harm
So come on, RAIN!!!"*

As the chickens squawked out the last word and froze in their positions, the whole farmyard went wild, all the animals grunting and cheering and stamping their hooves. But when Daisy looked up at the sky, it was just as sunny and blue as it had been for weeks.

"Don't worry," said Conker as Daisy climbed back onto the hay bales. "We've still got more to come, haven't we, Haze?"

"We certainly have," said Hazel. "Next up is Splat the Squirrel."

"Splat the Squirrel?"

"Yes," said Hazel, nodding enthusiastically. "Conker has to walk underneath the hay bales and we take it in turns to drop tomatoes on him. If anyone hits him on the head, they win a dandelion."

"What about Conker?"

"He gets sper-latted."

"Won't he mind?"

Hazel shook her head.

64

"He was the one who came up with it."

Daisy looked up and saw that Kevin Duck, Pauly Pig and Littlest Vole were sitting at the top of the hay bales with three very large tomatoes in front of them.

"Are you sure this is a good idea?" asked Daisy.

"Good?" said Conker. "It's genius."

He waved a paw at Kevin.

"You ready up there, Kev?"

Kevin waved back.

"Ready when you are!" he called.

"Just you be careful," said Daisy.

Conker began to walk beneath the hay bales, singing dramatically as he went.

"Derrrrr – dum!
Derrrrr – dum!

Dum dee-dump, dee-dump, dee-dump-dee
Dum dee-dump, dee-dump, dee-dump-dee..."

"And ... bombs away!" said Kevin. He pushed his tomato off the edge of the hay bale and it landed just behind Conker with a loud

SPLOT!

"Oooooh!" went the crowd.

"Missed!" shouted Conker.

Then he turned round and started walking back the other way.

"Dum dee-dump, dee-dump, dee-dump-dee
Dum dee-dump, dee-dump, dee-dump-dee..."

SPLOT!

went Pauly's tomato, bursting in front of Conker and splashing his face with tomato juice.

"Aaaaaah!" went the crowd.

"Yumsy," said Conker, licking his lips.
"That is one *tasty* tomato!"

Littlest Vole was the last to go.
Lots of his friends had stopped off
on their way to the pond because it
wasn't every day you got to see a vole
drop a tomato on a squirrel.

"You can do it, Littlest Vole!" they
shouted. "You can do it!"

Littlest Vole rolled the tomato right to
the very edge.

Conker tiptoed off again singing,

"Dum dee-dump, dee-dump, dee-dump-dee
Dum dee-dump, dee-dump, dee-dump-dee..."

Littlest Vole waited until Conker
was nearly underneath.

He took a deep breath.

Then he pushed.

Conker watched as a small grey spot on the ground grew bigger and bigger.

When he realized that it was the shadow of a large tomato, he stopped and looked up. Which was the same moment that a very large tomato hit him on the head and exploded.

THWALP! went the tomato.

"Hooray!" went the crowd.

Conker staggered around for a bit, cried, "Oooh, he got me!" then fell over backwards and stuck his feet in the air.

"Ooh, he got me! Ooh, he got me!" repeated the voles, giggling and crossing their legs and punching one another on the arm. One laughed so hard that a sunflower seed came out of his nose and he had to run behind the bushes before he had an accident.

"That was *fun*," said
Conker, getting to his feet
and flicking tomato pips from his
fur. "Can we do it again, please?"

"Not now," said Daisy, who had noticed
Hazel looking a little sad and guessed it
was because Conker was getting all the
attention. "It's nearly time for the donkey
race. Are you ready, Hazel?"

"Me?" gasped Hazel in amazement.

Daisy smiled.

"Yes, you," she said. "But you'd better not
beat me!"

Hazel squeaked, clapped her paws
together and scampered excitedly across to
where Hoofy and Straw were waiting.

"Oh, happy days," said Hoofy as Hazel
jumped onto his back and grabbed hold of
his ears. "Do you remember when we used
to have races like this down by the sea?"

"How could I forget?" replied Straw.
"Come on, Daisy. Up you come."

Daisy climbed onto his back and stroked his head.

"Happy days indeed!" he said.

Pandora Piglet trotted forward with a flag she had made from a bean stick and a piece of old sack.

"The race is from here to the water trough," she announced, raising the flag in the air.

Daisy looked over to where Rocky and the cows were standing, waiting for the race to begin. When Rocky saw her he put a hoof over his eyes and pretended he couldn't watch, which made Daisy giggle.

"Are you ready?" called Pandora. "On your marks, get set … GO!"

Daisy was still giggling as the two
donkeys set off across the yard, the animals
stamping and cheering all around them.
Out of the corner of her eye she saw Hazel
bouncing up and down, clinging on to
Hoofy's ears for dear life.

Daisy lifted one of Straw's ears and
shouted, "Slow down a bit," because she
really wanted Hazel to win. But Straw
couldn't hear her because of all the noise, and
before Daisy knew it they had reached the
water trough and all the ducks were cheering
while the cows said, "Well done, Daisy
dear," and "Super race, my love."
Daisy glanced over at Hazel
and saw how
disappointed
she looked,

so she leant over and whispered something in Rocky's ear.

"No problem," he said. "Leave it to me."

Meanwhile, in the centre of the yard, the Vole Display Team had begun their Special Performance. The smaller voles had climbed onto the bigger voles' shoulders and were singing, *"Dum diddle-um diddle-um dum-dum,"* as they got higher and higher, until at last they had formed a tall pyramid which teetered and tottered across the yard. Littlest Vole was on the very top and when he saw Daisy he waved excitedly.

"Look at me!" he called. "I can see the whole world!"

Rocky whispered something to the donkeys and then turned back to look at the voles.

"Good work, guys!" he called. "But don't move, 'cos we're going to finish off with the best Bucking Bronco Bonanza this farm has ever seen!"

"Yee-haw!" shouted Pauly Pig, although he wasn't sure why.

"Bucking Bronco Bonanza?" said Hazel. "What's that?"

"You just have to stay on the donkey and not fall off," said Daisy. "Whoever stays on longest is the winner."

"But—" said Hazel.

"Just hang on!" said Daisy and then Hoofy took off across the yard with Hazel hanging on to his ears.

"Yaaaaaaaah!" cried Hazel.

"Yaaaay!" shouted the animals, hardly able to believe that they were allowed to have so much fun in one single day.

As Hoofy bucked and kicked his way across the yard, Straw looked at Daisy.

"Ready?" he asked.

"Ready," said Daisy, grabbing the mane on the back of his neck. Straw trotted out into the middle of the yard and Daisy saw that Hazel was bouncing around but still hanging on tight.

"Well done, Hazel!" she called. "You're doing brilliantly!"

Then, as Straw kicked his back legs in the air, Daisy let go of his mane and slid carefully to the ground.

"Awwww!" went the animals. "Daisy's fallen off!"

"But Hazel hasn't!" shouted Daisy. "Look!"

Everyone turned to watch Hazel, who was clinging on to Hoofy's ear with one paw.

"The winner!" bellowed Rocky. "Hazel Squirrel is the all new Bucking Bronco Champion!"

"Hurrah!" cried the animals. "Hooray for Hazel!"

Unfortunately, a wasp chose that moment to land on Hoofy's bottom and sit down hard with its sharp stingy bit.

"Eee-yaw!" brayed Hoofy. "Eee-yaw, eee-yaw, eee-YOWCH!"

As he kicked his legs in the air, Hazel lost her grip and shot up into the sky.

"Ooooh," went the crowd.

"Uh-oh," said Straw.

Daisy looked up and saw Hazel falling towards the ground, flapping her arms as if she was trying to fly. Then Rocky bellowed, "Out of my way!" and galloped across the yard.

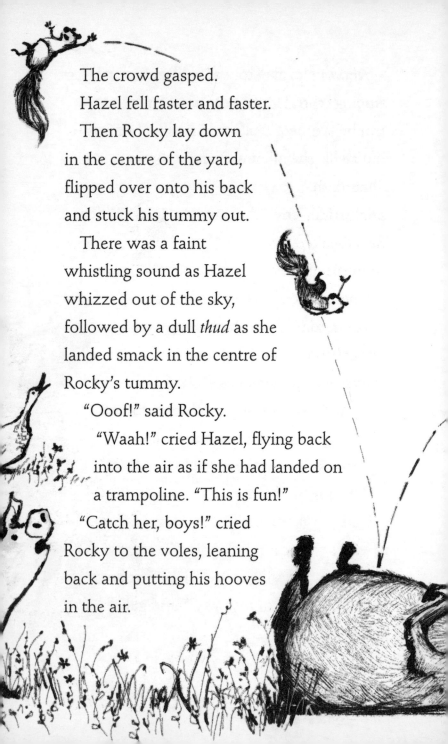

The crowd gasped.

Hazel fell faster and faster.

Then Rocky lay down in the centre of the yard, flipped over onto his back and stuck his tummy out.

There was a faint whistling sound as Hazel whizzed out of the sky, followed by a dull *thud* as she landed smack in the centre of Rocky's tummy.

"Ooof!" said Rocky.

"Waah!" cried Hazel, flying back into the air as if she had landed on a trampoline. "This is fun!"

"Catch her, boys!" cried Rocky to the voles, leaning back and putting his hooves in the air.

And as Hazel did a triple somersault
through the air Littlest Vole leant forward
from the top of the pyramid, grabbed her by
the arms and plonked her on his shoulders.

"And that, ladies
and gentlemen,"
he squeaked, "is
how it's done!"

There was a tremendous
cheer as Hazel stood at the top
of the pyramid and waved to
everyone down below.

Daisy turned to Rocky and smiled.
"Nice job, Rocky," she said.
Rocky winked and pointed
his hoof at her.

"Likewise, kid," he
said. "Likewise."

Puddles and Ponds

"All that running around has made me thirsty," said Rocky. "Think I'm gonna get me a nice long drink."

Dipping his head into the trough, he slurped up a huge mouthful of water. Then he stopped and furrowed his eyebrows as his cheeks seemed to do a little dance all by themselves.

"Bleauuuuugh!" he said, spitting the water out onto the grass.

As Daisy watched, three little newts
sat up in the middle of the newly formed
puddle and wiped their eyes.

"Guys, I am *so* sorry," said Rocky. "I had
no idea."

"Don't worry," said the oldest newt. "It
could happen to anyone."

"Although mainly to newts in a water
trough," said the middle one.

"I don't want to live here any more," said
the smallest newt. "I want to go back to our
pond."

Daisy looked at the three of them sitting
on the wet grass and realized that the plan
had failed. The sky was still blue, the pond
was still dry and the ducks and the newts
were still without a home.

"I'm sorry," she said sadly. "I don't know what else to do."

"Don't worry, my lovely," said a soft voice. "Things are never as bad as they seem."

Daisy turned to see Meadowsweet the mare standing behind her.

"Meadowsweet!" she cried, throwing her arms around her neck. "I didn't know you lived on the farm!"

"I don't," replied Meadowsweet, "but I heard a sparrow singing songs about you, so I thought I'd come over and say hello."

She looked at Daisy for a moment.

"Are you all right, my sweet? You seem so sad."

Daisy shook her head.

"I'm trying to make it rain," she explained, "but no matter what I do, nothing seems to work."

"Come and walk with me for a while," said Meadowsweet.

Daisy followed Meadowsweet towards the old oak tree where the grass grew long and the field mice slept in the shade of the branches.

"You see those hills over there?" asked Meadowsweet.

Daisy looked across at the rolling hills that rose above the valley.

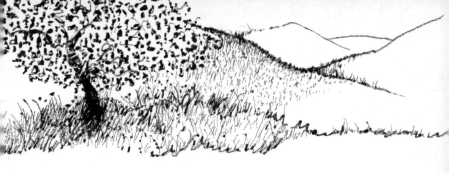

"Yes, I see them," she said.

"Many years ago when I was a foal," said Meadowsweet, "I decided that I wanted to climb to the very top of those hills. So I set off early one morning, thinking it would only take me a little while. But as the day wore on and the sun got hotter, I grew thirstier and thirstier. When I was halfway up, I was so tired that I wanted to give up. But I just kept going."

Daisy shook her head.

"I don't understand," she said.

"Just think of your troubles like climbing a hill," said Meadowsweet. "It might be hard at the moment, but it won't last for ever. And anyway, who wants to spend their life walking down a long straight road?

It's *much* more interesting to wander over hills and valleys."

Daisy rested her head against Meadowsweet's neck and stroked her mane.

"Did you make it to the top of the hill?" she asked.

Meadowsweet nodded.

"I got there just as the sun was going down," she replied. "And I found the sweetest patch of grass there that I ever tasted in my life."

She nuzzled Daisy's hair, her warm breath tickling Daisy's ear.

"So don't worry, my love," she whispered. "If the grass is dry, all you have to do is keep believing that one day the rain will fall."

* * *

"Excuse me," said a haughty voice to the animals gathered at the edge of the yard, "but would you mind keeping the noise down? Some of us have got work to do."

Daisy turned to see a sleek grey cat walk around the water trough with its tail in the air.

"Trixie!" said Daisy. "I'm afraid the Farm Afternoon is over. You've missed out on all the fun."

"Fun?" replied Trixie, regarding her with cool green eyes. "Is that what you call all this running about and making a racket?"

"Yes," said Pauly. "It is."

Trixie looked at him disdainfully. "And you are...?"

"A pig," said Pauly.

"I see," said Trixie. "Well, that says it all really, doesn't it?"

"Trixie, don't be mean," said Daisy.

"I'm not being mean," replied Trixie. "On the contrary, I think I've been extremely generous letting you use the farmyard for so long. But now I'd appreciate it if you'd all clear off as a few of us have some very serious business to attend to."

"Well, *really!*" said Doreen Chicken, storming off in a huff of feathers.

"What do you mean, *very serious business*?" asked Daisy.

"If you must know," replied Trixie, "it's our Cats' Annual General Meeting, which, as everyone knows, is the most important event of the year."

"Never heard of it," said Patsy.

"No offence," said Trixie, "but that's because you're a pig. Now if you don't mind, we've been planning this meeting all year and we don't want you lot hanging around and spoiling it."

"Just you hold your horses there, Whisker Face," said Rocky.

Trixie stared at him coolly for a few moments, then held up her paw.

"Talk to the paw, Bull Boy," she said, "'cos the cat ain't listening."

Flicking her tail in the air, she turned and walked daintily back to the centre of the yard, where the other cats were already starting to arrive.

"Bull Boy?" said Rocky. "*Bull* Boy?"

"Leave it, Rocky," said Phyllis. "She ain't worth it."

Rocky turned to look at Daisy and was surprised to see that she had a great big smile on her face.

"I don't see what's so funny," he said sulkily.

"Didn't you hear what she said about their Annual General Meeting?" replied Daisy. She pointed toward the cats, who had formed a big circle in the centre of the yard. "They've been planning it all year. Think about it!"

Rocky and the rest of the animals looked at each other in bewilderment.

One by one, they started to remember the things that people had said about planning events like school fetes and village days.

One by one, they looked up at the darkening sky.

Then, one by one, they began to smile.

"Cats are clever!" called Trixie.

"Miaow, miaow!" cried the circle of cats.

"Cats are handsome!"

"Miaow, miaow!"

"Cats are brave!"

"Miaow, miaow!"

"And cats are the finest animals in the whole wide world!"

"Miaow, miaow, miaow!"

"Oh puh-lease," said Conker. "Give me a break."

"Shh," said Daisy, trying not to laugh. "Look."

The cats were so busy congratulating one another that they hadn't noticed the clouds overhead.

"And of course," Trixie carried on, "everyone knows that it has been the driest summer for years. And you know why? Because the world knows that cats don't like water. And so the sky has smiled upon us and said, 'I shall not rain upon the wise and wonderful cats, because they are so fabulously great.'"

At that moment there
was a gust of wind, a flash of
lightning and a clap of thunder so loud
that it shook all the gates in the farmyard.

"Miaow?" said the cats, looking at one
another.

A fat droplet of rain landed in the middle of
the circle, followed by another, and another.

Trixie looked up at the sky.

"Ah," she said quietly.

Then with a tremendous roar, the heavens
opened and it rained and rained as
if it would never stop.

"Yes!" cried
the ducks and newts,
running for the pond.
"Result!"

"Yow!" cried the cats, running for shelter.

"Yay!" cried the rest of the animals,
running across the farmyard as a thousand
fat, wet raindrops fell from the sky and
burst all around them. "You did it,
Daisy! You did it!"

"We *all* did it!" replied Daisy,
dancing with the piglets in the rain.
"With a little help from those clever cats
of course!"

"Wipe your feet! Wipe your feet!" cried Martha as Pauly, Pete and Patsy tramped muddy trotter-prints through the middle of her living room. "Oh well," she sighed, scrubbing at the marks with her trotter. "At least no one's bored any more."

"Bored?" said Pauly. "I don't think I'll ever be bored again!"

And to celebrate he went back outside, put his head through the gate and went *clangety-clang-clang-clang*.

"Daisy, come and see what I've done," said Pandora Pig as Daisy ran in out of the rain. Daisy followed her to the corner of the pigsty and saw that, next to the picture of the duck pond, Pandora had drawn a brand-new picture. It was decorated with straw and flowers and it showed Daisy in the middle of the farmyard, surrounded by smiling animals.

"It's just how I wanted the world to be," said Pandora. "And thanks to you, Daisy, today it is."

As Daisy walked home through the long grass with Boom by her side, she looked back and saw a grey curtain of rain sweeping across the fields.

"It was a good day today, wasn't it, Boom?" she said.

Boom nodded.

"It was," he said. "A very good day indeed."

When they reached the edge of the meadow, he sat down in a puddle and rested his chin on the gate.

"Daisy," he said, "I was just wondering..."

Daisy leant over and patted the top of his head where the fur had gone all soggy. "What were you wondering, Boom?"

"I was just wondering ... you don't know any *sun* dances, do you?"

Daisy looked at the sky and the fields and the puddles in the lane.

She looked at the ducks in the distance, paddling around on their pond.

And she looked at Meadowsweet, bending her head to graze on the cool, sweet grass.

Wiping the rain from her eyes, she turned
to Boom and smiled.

"I'll see what I can do," she said.

Steve Voake is the author of five novels for older readers including *The Dreamwalker's Child,* and also writes the Hooey Higgins series for Walker. This is his fifth Daisy Dawson book. He says, "My daughter Daisy loves animals, and when she was little, she was always having conversations with them. I imagined what it would be like if they started talking back to her – and that's how Daisy Dawson was born!"

Steve lives in Somerset.

Jessica Meserve is the author and illustrator of the picture books *Small, Can Anybody Hear Me?* and *Bedtime without Arthur.* She has illustrated several other titles including *Drawing Together* by Mimi Thebo, *Grandad and John* by Jeanne Willis and the previous Daisy Dawson books. She says, "As a girl I wished I could talk to animals too. I love illustrating Daisy because she lets me have those adventures as a grown-up."